Baby Duck's New Friend

Frank Asch and Devin Asch

Gulliver Books
Harcourt, Inc.
San Diego   New York   London

www.harcourt.com

Gulliver Books is a trademark of Harcourt, Inc., registered in the
United States of America and/or other jurisdictions.

Library of Congress Cataloging-in-Publication Data
Asch, Frank.
Baby Duck's new friend/Frank Asch and Devin Asch.
p.   cm.
"Gulliver Books."
Summary: Baby Duck follows a rubber ducky down waterfalls,
through the woods, and far away from home, not realizing that he will
have to find his own way back.
[1. Ducks—Fiction.   2. Self-reliance—Fiction.]   I. Asch, Devin.   II. Title.
PZ7.A778Bc   2001
[E]—dc21   00-8189
ISBN 0-15-202257-0

First Edition
A C E G H F D B

Printed in Hong Kong

The illustrations in this book were drawn in pen and ink,
and colorized in Adobe Photoshop.
The display type was set in Berkeley Old Style.
The text type was set in Goudy Catalogue.
Printed by South China Printing Company, Ltd., Hong Kong
This book was printed on totally chlorine-free Nymolla Matte Art paper.
Production supervision by Sandra Grebenar and Ginger Boyer
Designed by Ivan Holmes

To my son
    —Frank Asch

To my father
    —Devin Asch

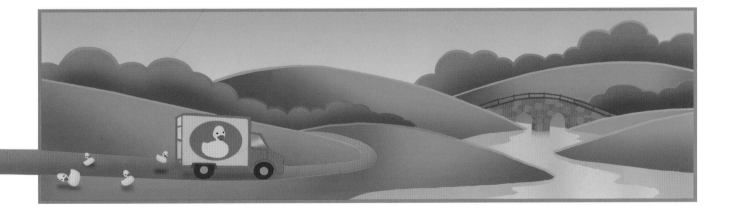

One sunny afternoon Baby Duck asked his mama if he could go for a swim by himself.

"Okay," replied Mama Duck, "but don't forget the rule: Ducklings can't go beyond the old stone bridge unless they are with someone who can fly."

"Don't worry," said Baby Duck. "I won't forget."

When Baby Duck reached the old stone bridge, he stopped and sighed. "If only I knew someone who could fly." Just then a small yellow duck landed beside him with a splash!

"Wow! You fly faster than my mama," cried Baby Duck. "Want to go exploring with me?" The yellow duck bobbed up and down. "Good!" said Baby Duck. "You go first." Without saying a word, Baby Duck's new friend turned and floated downstream.

When the yellow duck spun around, Baby Duck spun around. When it floated backward, Baby Duck floated backward, too.

"You don't talk much," said Baby Duck, "but you sure are fun!" Soon Baby Duck heard a strange roaring sound. Up ahead was something he had never seen before. "Oh my!" he cried. "The river is broken!"

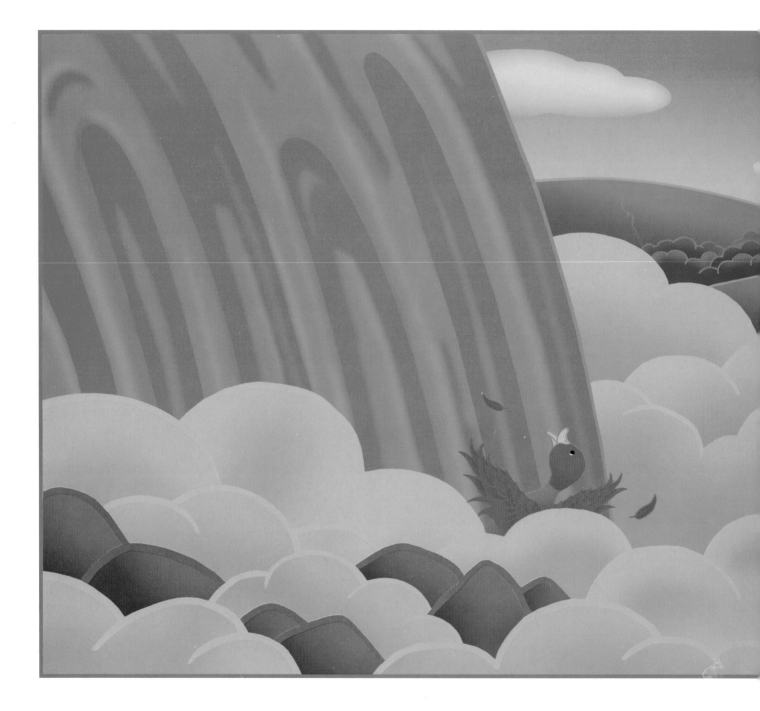

Down, down the two ducks plunged. At the bottom of
the waterfall, Baby Duck tumbled round and round.

But the yellow duck just bobbed up to the surface and sailed
on. Not a single feather was out of place.

After a while the river snaked through a dark forest. "This place is scary," said Baby Duck.

Around the next bend, Baby Duck saw a big red fox. "Watch out!" he quacked. "Mama said foxes are dangerous!" But the yellow duck just sailed on.

As the sun set, the river carried the two ducks to the sea.

Now Baby Duck was really frightened. He never dreamed water could be so *big*. "It's getting late, and I'm hungry," he quacked. "Please take me home." Suddenly a giant wave lifted Baby Duck into the air!

When the wave receded, Baby Duck saw a little boy walking down the beach. The boy ran over to the yellow duck and picked it up. "I'm going to take you home," he said. Then he put the duck in his bucket and walked away.

"Hey, what about me?" cried Baby Duck. "Who's going to take *me* home?"

For a long while, Baby Duck watched the moon rise. The waves breaking on the beach looked so big, he was afraid to go back in the water. "I never should have followed that yellow duck!" he shouted, and flapped his wings in anger. Suddenly his feet were no longer on the beach. "Oh my," he thought, "maybe I don't have to *swim* home after all."

Baby Duck ran toward the sea. When he reached the
water's edge, he flapped his wings and leaped into the air.

"Hey, look at me," cried Baby Duck as he rose higher and
higher into the night sky, "I'm flying!"

Baby Duck could see the river glistening in the moonlight.
"That's the way home," he quacked.

He followed the river through the forest, past the
waterfall, all the way back to the old stone bridge.

Finally he landed in the river with a splash and paddled
the rest of the way home.

As Baby Duck neared the nest, he quacked, "Mama, I'm home!"

Mama Duck was overjoyed to see her baby. Then she scowled. "Where have you been?"

"I swam all the way to the sea," replied Baby Duck.

"Did you break the rule?" asked his mama.

"Oh no," said Baby Duck. "I was with my new friend."

"Good," said Mama Duck, and she gave Baby Duck a minnow for his dinner.

"Now settle down and get some rest," said Mama Duck. "Tomorrow is going to be a *big* day."

"What's so special about tomorrow?" asked Baby Duck.

"Well," quacked Mama Duck softly. "Tomorrow I'm going to teach you how to fly!"

AUG 2001

1/02 ③

8/09 ㉓ 20

2015 ㉘

8/03

2020 34

/4

2021 34

12/05 ㉑

11/06 ①

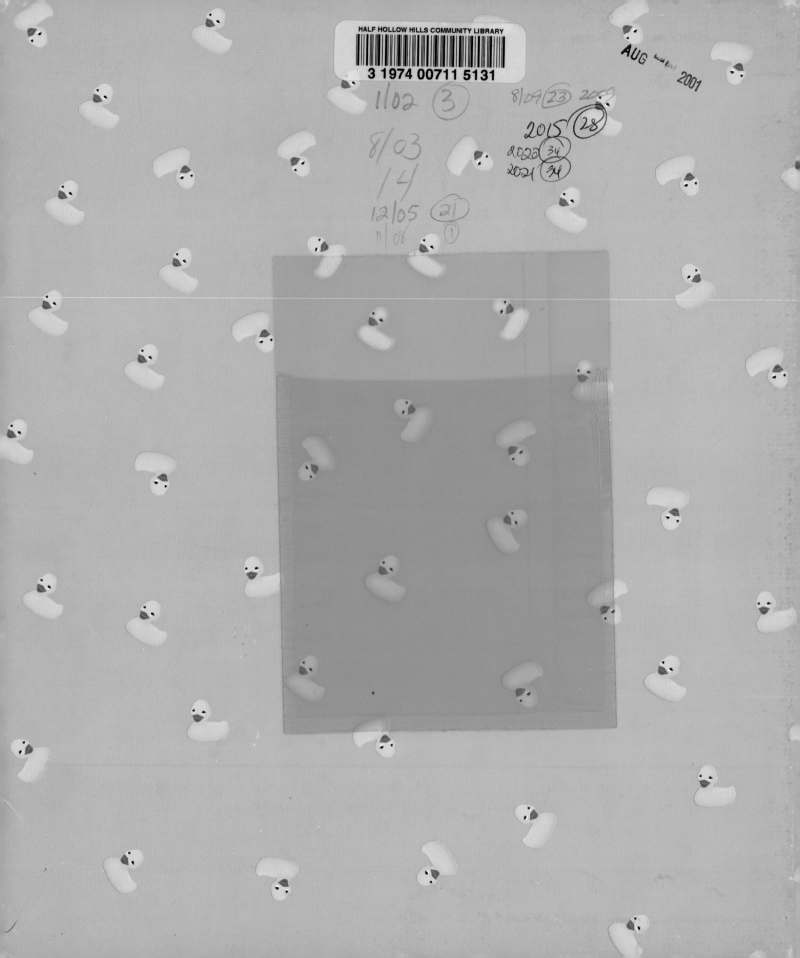